KARADI TALES

Whimsy

Annie Besant and Ruchi Mhasane

'What is
whimsy?'
she asked.

'Is it when I wear purple skirts and twirl yellow parasols,
or wear a boot front to back, all pink and laced with red?'

Mr. Prat looked at her with his piggy eyes. 'I'm whimsy,' he said, quite seriously, dabbing at his jam-smeared whiskers and licking his paws.

'I'm born of a pig
that met a rat and
fell in love.'

'Oh no!' she snorted, her bright
bushy tail flaring up.
You're not whimsy!

Whimsy is when I ride
my elephantamus across the park
and wave my handkerchief at the
mayor in the dark.'

Mr. Prat shook his big pink head. 'My snout is whimsy,' he said in a voice that rolled like bottles in the wind. 'It's a rat's snout with a pig's nose.

Have you ever seen anything as whimsical as that?'

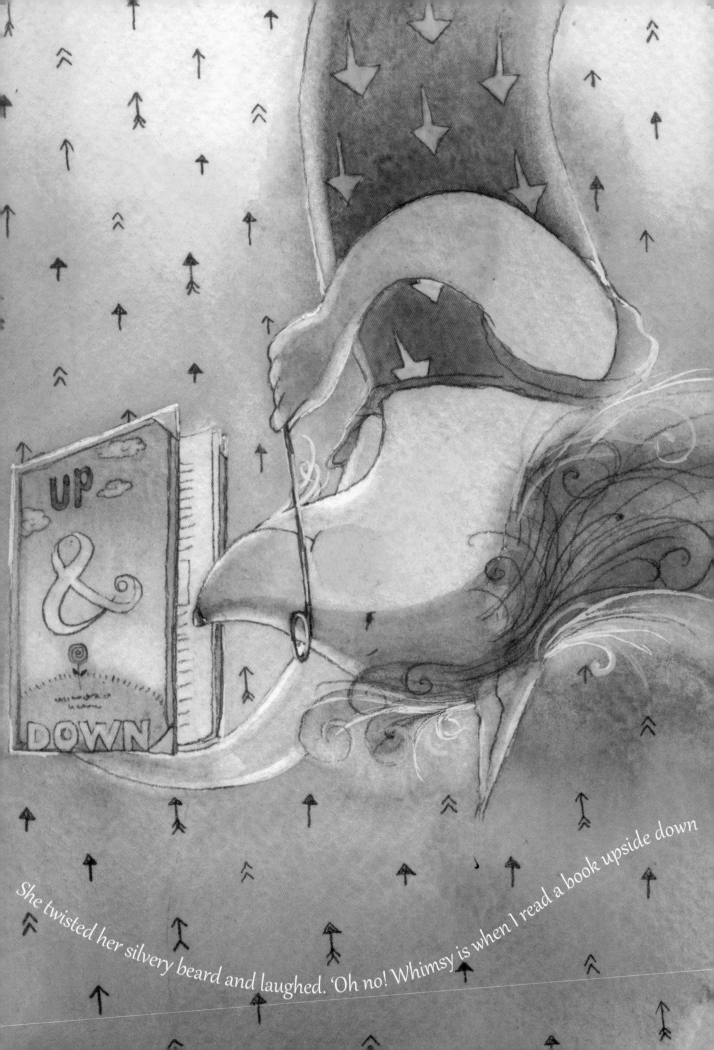

UP

&

DOWN

She twisted her silvery beard and laughed. 'Oh no! Whimsy is when I read a book upside down and do cartwheels till dawn. It's true, it's true, that is whimsy.

Mr. Prat folded his big blue neck-cloth and tucked it into his pocket. 'Come, come, Ms. Fox,' he said, 'My rat's tail and pig's body, my skinny feet and ears so scrawny, all plainly say that

I'm whimsy.'

Ms. Fox winked and shook her head. 'No, no, Mr. Prat,

whimsy is

when I wear a cat for a hat and feed it custard and cream with a silver spoon.'

Mr. Prat looked fondly at her and said, 'Sweet Ms. Fox, whimsy is when I wear pink pantaloons and ride a unicycle with my dog Blue.'

'Very well, then,' she said,
grinning ever so slyly.

'Since we are both whimsy,
Mr. Prat,would you like to
dance with me
forever by the light of the moon?'

Mr. Prat smiled till his rat's
teeth shone and kissed Ms. Fox
on her nose which was pointed
so much like his own.

'I thought you'd never ask.'

They wore pink
pantaloons, and went
to their wedding riding
a unicycle with their
dog Blue.

The guests ate plum
pudding and porcupine
pie and laughed to see
the whimsical couple.

'Do you think, Mr. Prat,' said Mrs. Prat laughing back at them, 'we can show them how to be whimsy too?'

And they did.

whimsy

Text: Annie Besant
Illustrations: Ruchi Mhasane

Karadi Tales Company Pvt. Ltd.
3A Dev Regency 11 First Main Road Gandhinagar Adyar Chennai 600020
Ph: +91 44 4205 4243 Email: contact@karaditales.com
Website: www.karaditales.com

Distributed in North America by Consortium Book Sales & Distribution
The Keg House 34 Thirteenth Avenue NE Suite 101 Minneapolis MN 55413-1006 USA
Orders: (+1) 731-423-1550; orderentry@perseusbooks.com
Electronic ordering via PUBNET (SAN 631760X); Website: www.cbsd.com

Printed in India
ISBN No.: 978-81-8190-305-1

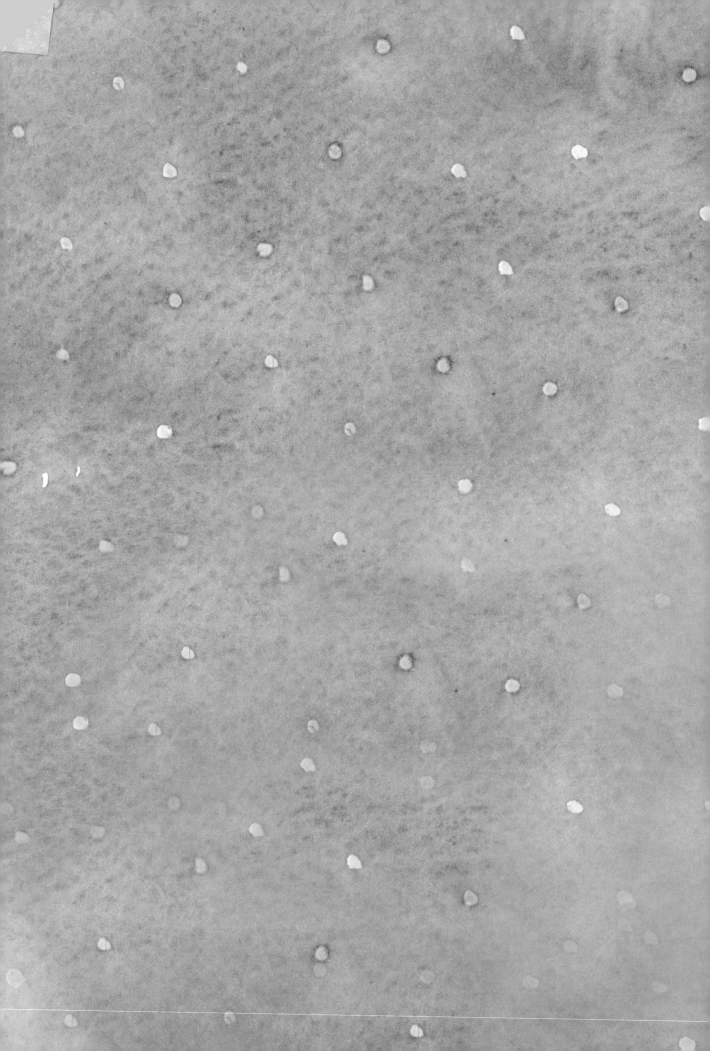